Posy the Puppy

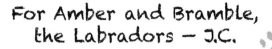

For Amber and Bramble,
the Labradors — J.C.

Text copyright © 2016 by Jane Clarke and Oxford University Press
Illustrations copyright © 2016 by Oxford University Press

All rights reserved. Published by Scholastic Inc., 557 Broadway, New York, NY 10012, *Publishers since 1920.* SCHOLASTIC and associated logos are trademarks and/or registered trademarks of Scholastic Inc. Published by arrangement with Oxford University Press. Series created by Oxford University Press.

The publisher does not have any control over and does not assume any responsibility for author or third-party websites or their content.

No part of this publication may be reproduced, stored in a retrieval system, or transmitted in any form or by any means, electronic, mechanical, photocopying, recording, or otherwise, without written permission of the publisher. For information regarding permission, write to Oxford University Press, Attention: Rights Department, Great Clarendon Street, Oxford, OX2 6DP, United Kingdom.

ISBN 978-0-545-87333-8

10   17 18 19 20

Printed in the U.S.A.   23
First edition, April 2016

Book design by Mary Claire Cruz

Posy the Puppy

Jane Clarke

Scholastic Inc.

Chapter One

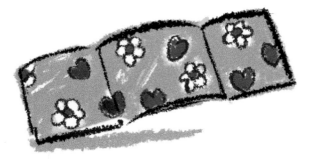

"Eek!" Peanut squeaked. "I can't reach the bandages—and Clover's ear is bleeding!"

"Don't panic, Peanut," Dr. KittyCat meowed calmly. She stretched out a paw and handed him a box of bandages from the supply closet.

Peanut turned to the little bunny next in line to see Dr. KittyCat. Clover

was sobbing loudly and holding a paw over one of his soft, furry ears.

"What happened to you, Clover?" Peanut asked.

A big fat tear rolled down the bunny's fluffy cheek.

"I caught my ear on a bramble," Clover wailed. Peanut opened Dr. KittyCat's *Furry First-aid Book* and made a quick note. The *Furry First-aid Book* was where they kept track of all the things they needed to remember about their patients.

"There, there, Clover," Dr. KittyCat meowed comfortingly as she washed and dried her paws. "Now, let me see."

Clover clamped both paws over his ear and cried even more.

"Dr. KittyCat does need to look at your sore ear," Peanut told him gently, "so she can make it better."

Very slowly, Clover took his paws away from his ear. Peanut handed him a tissue and helped him wipe away his tears.

Dr. KittyCat gently examined the small scrape on the bunny's ear. "The cut's not very deep," she murmured. "It will heal

quickly. But first, we need to clean it up."

"I know exactly what we need: a bowl of warm water, soap, and clean cotton-gauze swabs." Peanut raced around the clinic collecting things.

"Thanks, Peanut." Dr. KittyCat smiled. "You're a purr-fect assistant!"

Peanut stroked his whiskers happily as he watched Dr. KittyCat treat the cut on Clover's ear. Dr. KittyCat worked

calmly and steadily. She trickled clean
water over the cut, then gently sponged
away the dirt around it, carefully wiping
away from the wound and using a clean
piece of cotton-gauze swabs each time.

"You *are* a brave bunny," she told Clover as she patted his ear dry.

Peanut took the bowl and the used swabs away.

"Almost done," Dr. KittyCat announced. "It's time to put on a nice clean dressing."

Peanut showed the little rabbit the box of bandages. "Which one would you like?" he asked.

"That one!" Clover pointed to a big square bandage decorated with sparkly stars.

"Try not to touch it," Dr. KittyCat told Clover as she carefully stuck it on. "Your ear will heal by itself in a few days."

"It feels fine now!" Clover
announced, giving a tiny bunny hop.

"Well done," Peanut squeaked. "You
can have a special reward sticker!"

He handed
Clover a round
sticker that
said: "I was
a purr-fect
patient for Dr.
KittyCat!"

The young
rabbit stuck it on his sweater and
beamed with pride.

"Take care," Peanut and Dr. KittyCat
called after Clover as he skipped out of
the clinic with his cotton tail bouncing
behind him.

Peanut poked his head around
the door.

"There's still a long line of little animals waiting to see us," he told Dr. KittyCat. "They all have bumps, scrapes, and bruises."

Dr. KittyCat looked puzzled. "Why
are there are so many injuries today?"
she asked.

"It's the Paws and Prizes Field Day
tomorrow," Peanut reminded her, "and
some of the little ones have been
practicing too hard."

"Of course!" Dr. KittyCat exclaimed. "Posy told us all about it when she came in for her well-puppy checkup yesterday. She's hoping to win a prize." Dr. KittyCat giggled. "She was so excited, she raced around and around the clinic."

"Posy's the bounciest puppy I've ever seen," Peanut agreed. "I was amazed you managed to do her exam. I couldn't even get her to stand still."

He opened the door to Dr. KittyCat's clinic. "Come in, Nutmeg," he told a small guinea pig. "You're next . . ."

The guinea pig limped inside.

"What happened to you?" Peanut asked.

"I hurt my ankle!" the guinea pig
squealed.

"There, there, Nutmeg . . ." Dr.
KittyCat meowed kindly.

At last, everyone had been seen.

"What a busy day!" Peanut squeaked. "There are lots of notes to write up before we leave." He took the *Furry First-aid Book* to his desk.

"I'm going to start on my knitting," Dr. KittyCat said. "I found a pattern for a purr-fectly lovely hat."

Oh no! Peanut thought. *Please don't let it be for me.* He already had lots of things that Dr. KittyCat had knitted for him, and he wasn't sure he liked any of them very much.

Dr. KittyCat reached into her flowery doctor's bag. "That's odd," she meowed. "My bag wasn't closed all

the way—and I can't find the yarn. I
know I put it in here."

"Maybe it rolled out and got lost,"
Peanut said hopefully as Dr. KittyCat
carefully checked the contents of
her bag. "Scissors, syringe, medicines,
ointments, instant cold packs, paw-
cleansing gel, and wipes," she murmured.

"Stethoscope,
thermometer,
tweezers, bandages, gauze,
and reward stickers. Everything is
where it should be, except for my ball
of yarn . . ."

The telephone on Peanut's
desk began to ring. Peanut picked
up the handset.

"Dr. KittyCat's clinic.
How can we help you?"
Peanut asked, twirling
the telephone cord
so it curled tightly
around his paw.

"Just a moment . . ."

Brring!

Brring!

Peanut shook his paw out of the cord, and placed it over the mouthpiece.

"There's been an accident on the playing field," Peanut squeaked. "Posy's stuck in a tunnel on the agility course, and they think she's hurt!"

"Is the vanbulance ready?" Dr. KittyCat jumped to her feet.

Peanut nodded and held out the phone for her to take.

"It's such a shame," Peanut murmured. "Posy was really looking forward to the field day."

Dr. KittyCat took the phone. "Keep Posy still and calm," she meowed. "We'll be there in a whisker!"

Chapter Two

"Don't forget your bag!" Peanut clicked the flowery doctor's bag shut and thrust it into Dr. KittyCat's paws as they hurried out the door.

The vanbulance was parked next to the clinic, looking friendly and cheerful, Peanut thought, thanks to the bright flowers he had painted on it.

He hopped into the passenger seat, carefully pulled in his tail, and shut the door. He clicked on his seat belt, then slammed his paw against a button on the dashboard to sound the siren and make the light on the top of the vanbulance flash.

"Ready to rescue?" he squeaked, raising his voice above the siren.

Dr. KittyCat slammed her door shut, put on her seat belt, checked the mirrors, and took off the parking brake. "Ready to rescue!" she meowed.

The vanbulance sped through Thistletown. Peanut held tight to his seat belt as they bumped over Timber Bridge. Dr. KittyCat was driving so fast it made his tail bounce up and down and his whiskers quiver and shake.

"Eek!" he squealed as they rounded Duckpond Bend.

Dr. KittyCat held tight to the big steering wheel. "Don't panic, Peanut," she meowed, putting her paw on the accelerator. The vanbulance shook and rattled as they went faster and faster. "We're almost there."

Peanut shut his eyes.

There was a *scr-ee-eech* of brakes as Dr. KittyCat parked the vanbulance beside the playing field.

Peanut leaped out. At the far corner of the field there was an agility course with a seesaw, a balance beam, and a high jump. A few little animals were gathered around the canvas agility tunnel. Dr. KittyCat grabbed her flowery doctor's bag and hurried toward it. Peanut raced after her. As he got closer, he could hear a loud whimpering noise coming from inside the narrow tunnel.

Peanut and Dr. KittyCat peered into the opposite ends of the tunnel.

"I can't see anything," Peanut exclaimed. "Is Posy still in there?" he asked the group of young animals.

Sage, the owlet, shook her feathers.
"Yes," she hooted. "Posy's stuck in the
bend in the middle, and she won't
come out!"

Peanut raced around to the bend
in the tunnel and pressed his whiskers
against the canvas.

"Don't worry, Posy," he squeaked. "Dr. KittyCat is here. How are you doing?"

He could hear Posy take a deep breath inside the tunnel.

"Aooo!" she howled. "It hurts!"

The group of little bystanders gasped in concern.

Dr. KittyCat hurried over to where Peanut was standing. "Posy," she meowed. "Can you tell me where it hurts?"

There was a pause, and a lot of puppy-snuffling.

"It . . . it's my leg," Posy whimpered.

Dr. KittyCat pricked up her ears. "Posy should stay where she is until we figure out what's wrong with her leg," she whispered to Peanut. "But I'm not sure there will be enough room for me to examine her inside the tunnel."

"I'll go in and keep her calm while we both figure out the best way to treat her and get her out," Peanut suggested.

"Good idea," said Dr. KittyCat. "Take a cold pack with you." She opened her flowery doctor's bag.

"Oooh!" The curious crowd pushed forward to get a better look.

Peanut scurried into the tunnel. There was just enough sunlight

shining through the tough canvas for
him to make out a bundle of quivering
golden fur. The fluffy little puppy was
curled up in a tight ball in the gloom.

"I'm here now, Posy," he murmured.

A rubbery nose poked out of the
fur ball. "Ow!" she yelped.

"Posy," Dr. KittyCat meowed from outside the tunnel, "how did you hurt yourself?"

Peanut looked at Posy. She shook her head.

"She's not sure," Peanut squeaked. "Maybe her friends know."

"Did any of you see what happened?" Dr. KittyCat asked them. "Did Posy fall off the balance beam or the seesaw?"

There was a moment's silence.

"No," Sage hooted. "I was watching the whole time and I didn't see her fall. She just started limping and saying that she wouldn't be able to take part in Paws and Prizes tomorrow."

"That's right," Fennel, the fox cub, yipped.

"Right!" the other animals chorused.

"How badly was she limping?" asked Dr. KittyCat. "Did she put any weight on her bad leg at all?"

"She could walk on it a little," Fennel yipped. Peanut watched the shadow of Sage's head bob up and down as she nodded in agreement.

"Good," Dr. KittyCat meowed. "It doesn't sound like Posy has broken her leg."

"Which leg is it?" Peanut asked Posy.

"This . . . this . . . one," the puppy moaned, stretching out one of her back legs. "No, I mean this one." She nuzzled one of her front legs. "Ow!" she yelped.

"Posy can move her leg," Peanut reported, "but it seems to hurt at the joint."

"It might be a sprain. That can be very painful. Put the cold pack on her leg," Dr. KittyCat instructed.

Peanut shook and squeezed the pack to activate the cold.

"This will help," he said to Posy.

The tip of Posy's tail wagged a little.

"You're doing very well," Peanut said reassuringly as he held the cold pack against Posy's leg.

He could hear the sounds of commotion outside the tunnel.

"I'll bite it open," Fennel suggested.

"You'll break your teeth," Sage hooted. "I'll peck it open."

"You'll break your beak," Fennel yipped.

"I'll scratch it open with my claws," squeaked a little voice that Peanut recognized as Pumpkin, the hamster.

"You'll break your claws!" Sage and Fennel said together.

"I have a better idea," Dr. KittyCat meowed. Peanut looked up as her shadow fell across the canvas tunnel. He could tell she was opening her flowery doctor's bag and taking something out of it. She held up what looked like an enormous pair of shadowy scissors.

Aooo!

An
excited
ripple
went
through
the group
of animals
who were
watching. "Oooh!"

"She's taken out
her special scissors!"
Peanut squeaked
excitedly. "It's
Operation Posy!"

"Aooo!"
howled the anxious puppy.

Chapter Three

"Don't worry, Posy, I didn't mean an operation on *you*!" Peanut said. "Her special tough-cut scissors are for helping her get to her patients." He stared at the canvas walls of the tunnel. He could make out the shadowy outline of Dr. KittyCat as she held up her scissors.

"Peanut and Posy, I'll begin at

ground level and cut open the seam,"
Dr. KittyCat called to them. "Ready?"
Peanut looked at Posy. She
nodded slowly.

"You're being very brave," he murmured. "We're ready!" he squeaked.

Dr. KittyCat began to snip slowly and very carefully through the canvas.

"Do any of you know which leg Posy has hurt?" Dr. KittyCat asked.

"Her front leg," Pumpkin squeaked.

"No, it was her back leg," said Sage.

"Well, I definitely saw her limping on her front leg when she went across the balance beam," Pumpkin repeated.

Sage ruffled her feathers. "Posy was definitely limping on her back leg when she went across the seesaw," she told Dr. KittyCat.

"That's odd," Dr. KittyCat

murmured as she slowly snipped her way through the seam of the canvas tunnel.

Very odd, thought Peanut.

Inside the tunnel, Posy shuffled uncomfortably. "Ow!" she moaned.

"You'll be out soon," Peanut consoled her. "Try to stay still for just a little bit longer . . ."

Outside the tunnel, he could hear Dr. KittyCat asking more questions.

"Did anyone else notice anything wrong with Posy?" she meowed.

"I did!" quacked a duckling.

"That's my best friend, Willow!" Posy yapped. She pricked up her ears as Willow talked to Dr. KittyCat.

"Posy was upset when she was standing on the starting line," Willow quacked. "I heard her whimper."

"Did Posy start whimpering before she started limping?" Dr. KittyCat meowed.

"I think so," Willow said. "She

started off really slowly, too. She's usually very fast."

"Yesterday, she told me she was fast enough to win a medal," Dr. KittyCat murmured. "Something must have gone wrong before she started . . ."

In the tunnel, Posy fidgeted uncomfortably.

Peanut patted her paw. "Try to keep still," he squeaked.

"Poor Posy," Sage hooted. "She really wants to win a medal at Paws and Prizes tomorrow, but I don't suppose she can now . . ."

Posy whimpered.

"I'll be there in a whisker, Posy!"

Dr. KittyCat made a last snip with her tough-cut scissors and pulled back the canvas. Peanut blinked in the flood of bright sunlight.

Posy uncurled her head and stuck her little muzzle into the air.

"Aooo!" she howled.

"We'll make you feel better very soon, Posy," Dr. KittyCat meowed softly. She put the tough-cut scissors back in her flowery doctor's bag and snapped it shut, then turned to Posy's friends.

"Willow, Fennel, Pumpkin, and Sage . . . thank you very much, you've been a big help," she told them. "But

now I need you to stand back to give us some space while we take care of Posy."

The young animals backed away to give the vet more room.

"Posy," Dr. KittyCat meowed. "I need to take a look at your leg, so I can find out what's wrong and fix it. Are you ready?"

Posy slowly nodded her head.

"It's a bit of a puzzle," Dr. KittyCat whispered to Peanut, "but we'll figure it out."

Peanut nodded. "Sometimes being a doctor is just like being a detective!" he squeaked as he carefully lifted the cold pack away from the poor puppy's leg.

Chapter Four

"You are a brave puppy," Dr. KittyCat purred gently as she carefully examined Posy's leg.

"Her leg doesn't look swollen," Peanut commented.

Dr. KittyCat gently placed her furry paws on Posy's leg. "It doesn't

feel lumpy or hot, either," she agreed.
"Can you wiggle your toes, Posy?"

Posy wiggled all her toes.

"That's very good." Dr. KittyCat
smiled.

Posy slowly lifted her head. "It hurts," she whimpered.

"There, there, Posy," Peanut murmured. "Dr. KittyCat will find out what the problem is."

Dr. KittyCat nodded and held Posy's paw. She bent her head to Peanut's level.

"We should check to see if Posy has any other symptoms," she whispered to Peanut. "She might be suffering from shock."

"The first signs of shock are a quick pulse and cold skin," Peanut squeaked quietly into Dr. KittyCat's furry ear. "Posy does seem a little shivery . . ."

Dr. KittyCat nodded.

"I'm going to check your heart-beat," she told Posy as she held her paw on the pulse point on Posy's wrist.

"That's excellent, Posy!" Dr. KittyCat purred calmly. "Your heart is beating strongly and regularly. You're not in shock."

Peanut sighed with relief. "She must have been shivery because of the cold pack!" he squeaked.

"Now I'll check your breathing," Dr. KittyCat told Posy. "Pass me my stethoscope, please, Peanut."

Peanut very carefully pulled it out of the bag. Dr. KittyCat always made sure that she had her stethoscope with her, and she often used it to check her patients' lungs.

Dr. KittyCat popped in the earpieces and pressed the disc against Posy's chest.

"Everything sounds good," she told Posy. "Your breathing is fine. Not too deep and not too shallow, no rattling noises . . ."

She turned to Peanut. "All of Posy's vital signs are good. She's doing really

well. Just one more check before
we can allow her to move. I want to
take a good look at her eyes to make
sure she won't get dizzy."

Peanut took out something the size
and shape of a small flashlight.

"This is a special doctor's instrument for checking eyes," Dr. KittyCat explained to Posy as she held it close to the puppy's tear-filled eyes.

"That's purr-fect, Posy," she said. "Well done! You've passed all the tests and you can sit up now if you feel well enough."

The little puppy slowly sat up. Her ears drooped and she let out a yelp.

"This is all very odd," Dr. KittyCat said thoughtfully. She swished her striped tail. "I can't find anything wrong with Posy's leg," she told Peanut. "But she's still whimpering . . ."

"Her tail has lost its wag, too," Peanut squeaked, looking at the dejected puppy. "I wonder if she's telling us the truth about her leg . . ." he whispered.

Dr. KittyCat's ears pricked up. She blinked her bright eyes.

"We're a little puzzled, Posy,"
Dr. KittyCat meowed. "Does it hurt
anywhere else?"

Posy raised her muzzle to the sky.

"Aooo!" she howled. "Here!"
And she began to rub her stomach
with her paw.

"You *are* a good puppy for telling
us," Dr. KittyCat said. She turned to
Peanut. "Is there anything in your notes
about Posy ever having stomachaches?"
she asked.

Peanut flipped open the *Furry
First-aid Book*. He quickly read through
the sections that referred to Posy.

"There's no mention of any stomach

problems," he murmured. "And we know that Posy was fine and frisky when she came to the clinic yesterday."

"She certainly was," Dr. KittyCat meowed. "Bouncing everywhere, knocking over my bag, and even leaving chew marks on the table leg with her pointy puppy teeth!"

"Chew marks!" Peanut exclaimed.
"Of course! Puppies love to chew. It
must be something she's eaten. Posy!
Have you swallowed or chewed up
anything you shouldn't have?" he
squeaked.

Posy hung her head and looked at the ground.

"You can tell us," Peanut said encouragingly. "We won't be mad."

Posy sniffed. "I don't really have a sore leg," she confessed. "And I'm sorry for not telling the truth . . . but I didn't want to get into trouble."

Peanut and Dr. KittyCat looked at each other.

"We promise you won't get into trouble," Peanut reassured Posy. "It's really important to tell us what you did that made you feel sick."

"I . . . I knocked over Dr. KittyCat's flowery doctor's bag," Posy told them.

"That didn't make you feel sick, did it?" Peanut asked, puzzled.

"No . . . but then I nibbled at something." Posy groaned. "It was only a little nibble . . . but now I feel too sick to compete at Paws and Prizes." She let out a big sob.

"What did you nibble, Posy?" Peanut prompted her.

Posy's ears drooped so low they dragged on the ground. "I took a little nibble of something that rolled out of Dr. KittyCat's doctor's bag," she whimpered.

Peanut gasped. "Eek!" he squeaked. "What if she's eaten some of your pills,

Dr. KittyCat? That's really dangerous!
She could be poisoned! I should have
locked your bag away safely!"

"Don't panic, Peanut," said Dr.
KittyCat calmly. "All the pills are in
puppy-proof containers, and none of
my medicines are missing."

She turned to the little puppy.

"We're not angry with you, Posy. But we do need to know what rolled out of my bag, and what you took a little nibble of."

"It was a bit more than a nibble," Posy whispered.

"That's OK," Dr. KittyCat purred. "You can tell me."

"I . . . I chewed up one of your things!" Posy lifted her head and looked Dr. KittyCat in the eye. "I tried to spit it out, but I couldn't—and I couldn't swallow it, either. I haven't been able to eat anything since then, and I'm *so* hungry . . ."

"Hunger pangs can be very painful," Peanut said sympathetically.

"That would explain why your stomach hurts."

"We need to check out why you can't swallow," Dr. KittyCat meowed. "I'll have to look down your throat, Posy. Open wide . . ."

Posy opened
her jaws to show
two rows of tiny sharp
teeth and a big pink tongue.
"I will have to push your
tongue down, so that I can see," Dr.
KittyCat murmured. Peanut handed
her the tongue depressor, and Dr.
KittyCat pressed it down carefully on
Posy's tongue.

"There's something stuck at the
back of Posy's throat . . ." Dr. KittyCat
said slowly. "Take a look, Peanut."

Peanut peered into Posy's mouth. "I
can see it!" Peanut squeaked excitedly.
"I can see what's the matter!"

Chapter Five

Peanut could make out something small and purple at the back of Posy's throat.

"It's your knitting yarn!" Peanut squeaked.

"So that's where it went to!" Dr. KittyCat meowed. "Now we know what's wrong! No wonder you're feeling sick. Can you give a really big cough?"

Posy coughed. The ball of yarn shot out onto the ground.

"Good job!" Peanut and Dr. KittyCat exclaimed together.

Woof! Posy leaped to her feet, wagging her tail.

Her friends hurried back over. "Yay!" they cheered.

"Posy is feeling better already," Peanut said. "She'll be fine. We just need to keep an

eye on her for a little while. She'll see
you later."

"Bye, Posy!" Willow quacked.
"Get well soon!"

Peanut led the way to the
vanbulance.

"I've never seen the inside before," Posy yapped excitedly.

"You'll love it!" Peanut said. "We do!" He slid the side door of the vanbulance open.

"Wow!" Posy woofed. "It's got polka-dotted curtains and cushions and everything!"

Peanut settled Posy on the bench

seat beside the table. He tucked a blanket around her. In a moment, little puppy snores echoed around the vanbulance.

"I feel much better," Posy said when she woke up from her nap. "I should go back home now, before anyone gets worried."

"Remember to be very careful about what you chew and swallow," Peanut told her as he slid open the door.

"I will," Posy promised. She paused at the door. "I can take part in Paws and Prizes tomorrow, can't I?"

"Of course!" Peanut and Dr. KittyCat said together.

Posy yapped for joy. Then, suddenly, her ears and tail drooped.

"You're not feeling sick again, are you?" Peanut squeaked, worried.

"The tunnel," Posy howled. "It's ruined because of me. There can't be an agility course without an agility tunnel. I've ruined the whole day for everyone!"

"I've already
thought of that,"
Peanut said. "It's
nothing that a mouse with
a needle and some surgical thread can't
fix! I keep an emergency supply in
the vanbulance."

"Yay!" Posy jumped up and down,
wagging her tail. "Will you come and
watch me tomorrow?" she
asked. "Pleeease?"

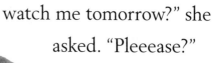

"Yes!" Dr.
KittyCat laughed.
"We'll be here
anyway—we're
providing the first aid!

In fact," she meowed, "we might as well stay here tonight."

Posy's eyes opened wide as she looked around the vanbulance. "But where do you sleep?" she asked. "I don't see any beds."

"The table folds away, and then this bench turns into a bed for Dr. KittyCat," Peanut explained. "And I have my very own room up here." He scrambled up to a little cabin built into the roof and waved down at Posy. "I have my own bed and desk and chair and everything!"

"Cool! Thanks for showing me," Posy yapped as she waved good-bye. "I wish I could live in a vanbulance!"

Chapter Six

It was the morning of Paws and Prizes Field Day, and Peanut was up early to mend the agility tunnel.

"It looks as good as new!" said Dr. KittyCat, admiring Peanut's row of tiny, neat stitches in the canvas. "You'd make a very good surgeon, Peanut."

Peanut's tail twitched happily as he gathered up his needle and thread. "We better get out of the way," he squeaked. "The competitions start soon."

Dr. KittyCat and Peanut made their way back to the vanbulance. Peanut set up the Furry First-aid sign, and Dr. KittyCat put her flowery doctor's bag beside it. They each got a folding chair from the vanbulance.

"It's a lovely sunny day," Dr. KittyCat said, "and no one has needed first aid yet." Then she winked at Peanut and said, "It would have been the purr-fect moment to do some knitting if my yarn hadn't gotten eaten!"

Peanut picked up his pencil, opened the *Furry First-aid Book*, and began to write up the notes he had made about Posy. "You were very smart to figure out what was wrong with Posy," he told Dr. KittyCat. "It was a difficult case."

"Very tricky," Dr. KittyCat agreed. "I couldn't have done it without your help, Peanut."

Peanut grinned such a big grin that his whiskers fluttered.

Just then, a big cheer echoed across the playing field. Peanut and Dr. KittyCat looked up.

"Posy's about to start the agility competition," Dr. KittyCat said, smiling.

"I can't watch," Peanut squeaked as Posy tiptoed along the balance beam, raced up and down the seesaw, and dashed in and out of the agility poles. She squirmed through the mended tunnel and leaped over the high jump.

Even from a distance they could hear her excited *yap-yap-yap*s as she raced across the finish line.

"Whew!" Peanut put his nose back in his notes. "She didn't hurt herself, and she made good time. She might even get a blue ribbon."

"We'll have to wait and see," purred Dr. KittyCat.

Half an hour later, the loudspeaker crackled to life. "Congratulations to everyone who took part in the agility competition," it announced. "The winners are . . . in third place, Fennel! In second place, Posy! And in first place, Nutmeg! We invite Dr. KittyCat and Peanut to present the blue ribbons."

"That's us!" Peanut snapped the first-aid book shut and Dr. KittyCat stood up and stowed her flowery doctor's bag safely in the vanbulance. Then they hurried to the podium where the winners were waiting. Posy was standing there proudly, wagging her tail so hard it was a blur.

Peanut passed Dr. KittyCat the blue ribbons, and she presented them to the winners. Then, as Dr. KittyCat and Peanut were leaving the podium, Posy ran after them.

"Thank you," she yapped, proudly patting her blue ribbon with

her paw. "I won this blue ribbon because you made me better!"

"You're welcome, Posy!" Dr. KittyCat meowed.

"I'm hoping to get another blue ribbon, too," Posy whispered to Peanut.

The loudspeaker crackled again. "The next race is the sack race," it announced.

"Yippee!" Posy squealed, bouncing up and down on all fours.

Dr. KittyCat and Peanut stood
back as a crowd of overexcited puppies
and kittens raced to the starting line and
wiggled into their sacks.

"Ready . . . set . . . go!" boomed the
voice from the loudspeaker.

There was an eruption of squeals,

squeaks, and howls as the little animals bumped and tripped and crashed into one another.

"Dr. KittyCat and Peanut are needed at the first-aid station," said the loudspeaker voice.

"Uh-oh!" squeaked Peanut.

A long line of animals with minor bumps, bruises, and cuts was waiting at the vanbulance.

"We would like to thank Dr. KittyCat and Peanut for providing our first aid today," the announcer went on. "They make a great team."

Peanut and Dr. KittyCat grinned at each other.

"We do," Dr. KittyCat meowed as she took her flowery doctor's bag out of the vanbulance and put it down beside her. "Pass me the bandages, Peanut!"

The end

What's in Dr. KittyCat's bag?

Here are just some of the things that Dr. KittyCat always carries in her flowery doctor's bag.

Tough-cut scissors

These special scissors are strong but not sharp! Dr. KittyCat uses them in first-aid emergencies to cut through clothing or other materials without harming her patients. She also uses them for cutting bandages.

Stethoscope

With a stethoscope, Dr. KittyCat can listen to sounds from inside her patients' bodies. At the end of the stethoscope there is a rounded "bell" side and a flatter "diaphragm" side, and each side is used for listening to different sounds, such as a heartbeat or the sound of breathing.

Cold pack

Dr. KittyCat always makes sure she has enough cold packs in her bag. She uses each pack only once by squeezing it gently so that it quickly becomes cold enough to soothe bumps, bruises, strains, and sprains.

Tongue depressor

Peanut thinks tongue depressors look like Popsicle sticks! But in fact, Dr. KittyCat uses these flat, thin, rounded pieces of wood to gently press down a patient's tongue so that she can have a better view of his/her mouth and throat.

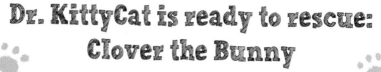

Dr. KittyCat is ready to rescue:
Clover the Bunny

Dr. KittyCat, Nutmeg, Pumpkin, and Peanut raced toward Clover's cries. At the far side of the clearing, there was a pile of wood near the base of an old tree trunk.

"He dropped his firewood," Pumpkin said, worried. "Something must have happened to him!"

"Waah!" Clover wailed again. Dr. KittyCat's ears pricked up. Peanut glanced around wildly, but all he could see was shadows.

"I've spotted him!" Dr. KittyCat exclaimed. She pointed to a little mound of fur huddled up in the dappled light. It was Clover, quivering from his whiskery nose to his cotton tail.

"Waah!" Clover cried. "Waah!"

"Dr. KittyCat's come to rescue you, Clover," Peanut squeaked. "Everything will be all right now."

Don't panic, Peanut!

A note from the author:

Jane says...

"Once, my dog, Amber, had a big pink spot on her side, and she looked very, very upset. I panicked, like Peanut, the mouse in this story, thinking it was a bad injury, but it turned out to be just a patch of bubble gum stuck to her fur!"

See you next time!

Visit Friendship Forest, where animals can talk and magic exists!